Spatz

THE SCRATCHING SOUND

Sherry W. Fair

THE SCRATCHING SOUND

Spatz

Sherry W. Fair

Illustrated by Jarrett Rutland

Junaluska Resources
PROVIDENCE HOUSE PUBLISHERS
FRANKLIN, TENNESSEE

Printed in the United States of America

09   08   07   06   05   1   2   3   4   5

Library of Congress Control Number: 2005922663

ISBN: 1-57736-348-5

Illustrations by Jarrett Rutland

Cover design by Joey McNair

238 Seaboard Lane • Franklin, Tennessee 37067
www.providence-publishing.com
800-321-5692

Ruff!

My name is Stonerhaven Carolina Spatz. You can call me *Spatz*.

I am a Shetland Sheepdog.

My ancestors herded sheep on the Shetland Islands.

Some people call me a Sheltie.

You can call me a Sheltie, but I like my name.

Do you remember my name?

Shelties have many color groups.

Some favorites are Sable, Blue Merle, Tricolor, Bi-Black, and Bi-Blue.

Do you have a color?

My color is mostly black and white with a little bit of brown.

Can you see the mask on my face? I am called a Tricolor.

Can you guess why?

I like to play.

Today, I want to play with the gray squirrel.

Spatz had finished his breakfast and sat looking out through

the back door glass. He looked up high in the trees,

and he saw something move . . . *f a s t.*

Spatz began to move fast too.

He jumped and turned in circles.

And he barked,

"I have to go out!"

When the door opened,

he flew down the steps

and ran through the grass

toward the tallest tree.

Close to the tallest tree, he stopped and lay down.

And his eyes watched. *Spatz* was very still and quiet.

His ears listened to the birds sing.

He felt the wind blow his long fur.

A scratching sound told *Spatz* to get ready.

He stood low to the ground

and pointed a paw toward

the scratching sound.

Spatz was ready to go, but he didn't move around.

Spatz listened and watched
Gray Squirrel

C
I
R
C
L
I
N
G

down the
tree trunk to
the ground.

Gray Squirrel sat up tall, shook his bushy tail,

and hopped to pick up an acorn.

Gray Squirrel hopped.

And *Spatz* hopped.

Gray Squirrel saw *Spatz* and ran fast.
Spatz ran fast after Gray Squirrel.
He ran and he ran with
his tail straight behind.

He looked like an arrow
flying near to the ground.

Spatz ran so fast and close to Gray Squirrel that he could almost nip at Gray Squirrel's toes.

Spatz ran to the left of Gray Squirrel.

And then, he ran to the right of Gray Squirrel.

All of a sudden,

Gray Squirrel

F L E W

into the *AIR!*

And *Spatz* *flew*

. . . *p a s t* the tallest tree.

Spatz stopped quick and looked, but he didn't see

Gray Squirrel any more.

He looked right and left, and he turned around.

But the little gray squirrel

wasn't on the ground.

Spatz waited, and he listened

to *the scratching sound.*

Gray Squirrel climbed up to a nest in the tallest tree.

Spatz sat in the shade of the tallest tree.

Gray Squirrel was up, so *Spatz* lay down.

Spatz was very still and quiet.

His ears listened to the birds sing.

He felt the wind blow his long fur.

Spatz smiled as he rested in the shade on the ground.

And he waited once again for *the scratching sound.*

RUFF!

ABOUT SHELTIES . . . AND SPATZ!

The Shetland Sheepdog, called the Sheltie, is one of the most versatile breeds of dogs living today. These dogs are beautiful, intelligent, agile, sturdy, loving, and devoted to their families. Shelties are willing to learn anything that their owners care to teach them! Spatz, the star of this book series, was born at the Stonerhaven Sheltie Kennel in Roebuck, South Carolina, on July 24, 2003. His mother is a blue merle champion named Tilly and his father is a tricolor fellow called Trigger. Spatz was one of three tricolor puppies. He has a brother named Fritz and a sister named Bella. Spatz was named for old-fashioned shoe coverings called spats. The more you read about Spatz, the more you love him!

Christina Stoner
AKC Obedience Judge, Rally Judge,
CGC Evaluator, Therapy Dog INC Tester

ABOUT SPATZ'S BREEDER

The Stonerhaven Sheltie Kennel, owned by Robert and Christina Stoner of Roebuck, South Carolina, was formed in 1968. The Stonerhaven Shelties are multi-faceted dogs. They compete in breed competition, obedience classes, agility, and rally trials. Stonerhaven Shelties have achieved top rankings in all venues of competition, including a Best In Show champion (1994) that was the number one winning Sheltie in the United States and the first Sheltie to ever advertise for the Purina Dog Food Company. In addition to showing dogs, the Stoners take their registered Therapy Shelties to visit hospitals and nursing homes to bring good cheer and happy wagging tails to shut-ins.

ABOUT THE AUTHOR

A teacher, writer, and storyteller, Sherry Fair has a bachelor's degree in English from Columbia College. Over the past twenty-six years, she has taught school and helped students ranging in age from four to eighty-four to create and develop characters and stories. They have presented their work in written form and on stages for churches, schools, summer workshops, and community events.

Sherry now shares her own characters and stories in a book series that features her Sheltie, Stonerhaven Carolina Spatz. Sherry is a member of the Aiken chapter of the South Carolina Writers Workshop and the Society of Children's Book Writers & Illustrators.

For twenty-three years, she has traveled with a Sheltie at her side. Sherry and Spatz make their home in the North Carolina Blue Ridge Mountains and the South Carolina Midlands with Sherry's husband, Dr. Hal Fair. To schedule Sherry and Spatz for a visit with your group, or to order books online, go to www.spatzbooks.com.

ABOUT THE ILLUSTRATOR

Jarrett Rutland has both won awards and taught students who won awards . . . which is impressive, since he was only in fifth grade when he taught the other award-winning students. Later, as a high school student, he was awarded the National Congressional Art Award for the state of Alabama, and as a college junior, he received his school's Illustration Department Award. Jarrett has a bachelor of fine arts degree from the Maryland Institute College of Art and has studied art in Canada and France.

Jarrett resides in Alabama and North Carolina, where he illustrates children's books like the Spatz book series. He also produces commissioned works, designs greeting cards and stationery, and has developed a comic strip. He is a member of the Society of Children's Book Writers & Illustrators.

Spatz is a registered AKC Shetland Sheepdog—also called a Sheltie. He is sixteen inches tall. Spatz has a white ruff around his neck and four white legs. His middle is black, and his tail is black with a white tip. His hair is thick and long, and he looks like he has a mask on his face.

Spatz likes to get dirty and play hide-and-seek. He likes to run, fetch balls, and catch Frisbees. He likes to eat. And he likes to blow bubbles under water with his nose.

Spatz lives in the North Carolina Blue Ridge Mountains and the South Carolina Midlands. He loves to ride in a truck, on a boat, and in his shiny red parade car to see his friends.

If you visit or live in the Carolinas,
you never know
but that you just might see
Sheltie
Spatz
on the go!

*****

To find out more about Spatz and for more Spatz books, go to . . .
www.spatzbooks.com

Join Spatz in his shiny red parade car traveling Lakeshore South to Lakeshore North as he celebrates the Fourth of July in his next book, *The Best Parade Day.*